SHOCKED IN CHICAGO

RAMBLING RV COZY MYSTERIES, BOOK 23

PATTI BENNING

SUMMER PRESCOTT BOOKS PUBLISHING

CHAPTER ONE

The only thing separating Tulia Noble from home was a single lake. Granted, it was one of the largest lakes in the world; Lake Michigan, a lake that would have been considered an inland sea if it hadn't been freshwater. Still, as she stood in the balcony window of the newest suite they were staying in, she couldn't take her eyes off of the shining water.

She felt bad for not taking the time to visit Michigan on her road trip, but she had grown up there. She had already written a blog post about it, and just a couple of weeks ago, she had seen the most important people from her hometown—her parents.

Tulia could make the time to visit Michigan whenever she wanted, but right now, they were on a schedule. A schedule they were already behind on.

"Which room do you want?"

The question came from Olivia, her traveling companion and videographer, and the person who was nominally in charge of keeping them on task. Olivia worked for the studio that had contracted with Tulia to make the travel documentary they were currently working on. It was an ambitious project; an episode for every state, starting with the ones she hadn't visited yet. It had taken them two months to travel from Massachusetts, where her new home with her husband, Samuel, was, to Chicago, which they had just arrived in an hour ago.

And they had only now gotten up to their suite. Their *shared* suite. The delay was thanks to a double booking on the hotel's end, and a long wait while the staff tried their best to make another suite appear out of nowhere. Although Olivia's stipend only covered the fee for the base room of the hotel's cheapest room, Tulia had gotten into the practice of booking them both suites. She didn't mind spending a little extra money for her friend, and it wouldn't have felt right to enjoy a suite while Olivia slept in a tiny room several floors beneath her.

She supposed they could both have gotten base rooms, but she had won the lottery—literally. She kept a tight rein on her finances, but there were some things it was fun to splurge on. Plus, she had learned that hotels were much more likely to make an exception to their no pets policy when the person asking for that exception had booked their most expensive rooms. Cicero, her African Grey parrot, was one part of her life where she didn't hesitate to spend, and traveling with him was already difficult enough without only staying at the places that advertised that they were pet friendly.

She turned away from the window to respond to Olivia as she walked over to Cicero's cage to open the door and let him climb on top of it. "It doesn't matter to me, you can choose."

The hotel hadn't been able to solve the double-booking issue, but they had been able to change the booking to a suite with two bedrooms, which as far as Tulia was concerned, was just as good. She didn't mind sharing with Olivia, but when they were going to be traveling together for months on end and saw each other day in and day out, it was nice for them both to have their own space where they could retreat and relax in the evenings.

She couldn't complain about the suite itself. It was a large, modern room on the upper floor of a ten-story hotel that looked out across Lake Michigan from the edge of Chicago. The city was all around them, but the room's soundproofing was good enough that she couldn't hear a thing. The suite's floors were a dark, faux wood, and the rug and furniture in the living room were white — a daring color for a hotel room— with abstract art hanging on the walls that lent the room a splash of color. The ceilings were high, ten feet rather than eight, with exposed beams, and the bedrooms and bathrooms were also modern and sleek. The entire suite felt like a converted warehouse loft, though she knew the building had been built new a few years ago.

The generous balcony looked out over the lake, which was the only thing she could see unless she looked directly down at the road and shoreline. But her favorite part of the suite was a reading nook in a window next to the balcony. There was a padded bench and some throw pillows with space for someone to sit. While Olivia decided which bedroom she wanted, Tulia tossed the throw pillows onto the couch and opened her suitcase to pull out an old towel, which she laid down on the padded bench.

Then, she walked back over to Cicero's cage and asked him to step up on her hand before carrying him over to the nook by the window. She placed him down on the towel and watched as he waddled over to the glass to touch it with his beak and a waggle of his bright red tail feathers. It was the perfect view for a bird, and she had a feeling the little window nook would become his favorite spot while they stayed here.

She shot the balcony door a distrustful glance and decided to pick up some sticky notes when they went out to remind them both not to open the door if Cicero was loose in the room. The last thing she needed was for him to fly out of a window from ten stories up. With that much height, he might be able to make it all the way across the lake to Michigan.

"I'll take this one!" Olivia called as she poked her head out of the bedroom door nearest the kitchenette.

Eager to begin unpacking, Tulia rezipped her suitcase and dragged it and her other bags through the bedroom door opposite Olivia's. They left their doors open and chatted as they settled in. They had a week there, and it was going to be a busy. She and Olivia had both taken a handful of breaks over the past couple of months, and the studio wasn't happy about it. They wouldn't say as much, not to Tulia's face since it wouldn't take much for her to get out of the contract if she decided she didn't want to work with them, but Tulia took the contract she had signed seriously, and she also didn't want Olivia to get in trouble at her job. All of that meant they had a lot of catching up to do and needed to get some impressive footage of Chicago to make up for the time they had taken off.

While it was stressful to juggle everything the studio wanted them to do, on the upside, most of what they wanted them to do was fun. It was almost like a scavenger hunt, where they had to do some research to find the best local restaurants and little-known attractions that they then got to explore.

Tulia had been to Chicago before, albeit briefly, and was looking forward to seeing more of the city. Most of the places she and Olivia had stopped during their road trip were either rural or small to medium-sized towns. Of the handful of cities they'd visited since they left Massachusetts, Chicago was easily the largest. Tulia preferred the quieter, slower life of small towns, but there was something invigorating about the city. Even better, their hotel was in one of the more walkable parts of the city, which meant she wouldn't need to navigate the busy streets with a car in order to explore.

As she finished folding her pajamas in the top drawer of the dresser opposite her bed, her stomach growled. They hadn't eaten since breakfast, which had been a bowl of cereal and a banana for Tulia. Bad traffic and then the delay once they got to the hotel had also delayed their lunch, and now it was almost dinnertime.

"Hey, Olivia? What do you want to do about food tonight? I could place an order for room service or takeout if you want to stay in." She poked her head out through her bedroom door as she spoke and saw Olivia do the same from across the living room. The younger woman bit her lip for a moment as she thought.

"I'd kind of like to eat out somewhere, if you don't mind. It's been a while since I've gone to an actual sit-down restaurant instead of eating fast food or hot dogs and beans I cooked over a fire."

"Sure, we can go out," Tulia said. "I'm done unpacking, so I'll put Cicero away and start looking up local restaurants while you finish getting ready."

Before putting her bird in his cage, Tulia cleaned out his water bowl and refilled it with fresh water, then added a scoop of pellets to his food bowl. She dropped an almond in as well, to bribe him since she knew he wasn't ready to go back in his cage yet. He gave her an unhappy look as he waddled across his perch to get his treat.

"Sorry, buddy," she murmured as she latched his cage door. "I know you've been cooped up all day. You can spend the rest of the evening out once we get back, I promise."

He picked the almond up in his scaly foot and began to break pieces off with his beak, which told her he wasn't too upset. She turned his cage a little so he had a good view through the window, then sat down on the couch and took out her cell phone so she could browse the local food offerings.

She was stunned by just how many there were. While she loved Loon Bay, the little Massachusetts town she and Samuel called home, it boasted a grand total of three restaurants, one of which didn't even have a dining area. In Chicago, the number of food options in a three block radius were a little overwhelming.

She was so hungry that everything looked good, which made it hard to choose. She turned her phone's screen off and put it down, deciding there were enough options nearby that she didn't have to choose now. They could set off from the hotel on foot and run into ten different places to eat before they had crossed two blocks. Maybe it would be easier to choose when they could see the restaurants in person and smell the delicious scents of what they were offering.

CHAPTER TWO

As soon as Olivia was ready to go, Tulia got her shoes on and grabbed her purse. She paused to make sure the door to their suite was locked, not wanting to take any chances with Cicero, then the two of them walked to the elevator together and took it down to the ground level. The hotel's lobby was quiet and peaceful, but as soon as they stepped outside, the noises and smells of the city washed over them. The air smelled a little fishy from the lake, which mixed with the scents of car exhaust and smoke from nearby restaurants to create an effect that wasn't exactly pleasant but wasn't terrible either. The hotel was on a corner of a block, and the road that followed the lakeshore was busy. Thankfully, the road it intersected with wasn't quite so bad. They turned onto the quieter road and followed the sidewalk away from the lake.

There were still cars going by, but it was a quieter two-lane road instead of the busy four-lane road at the front of the hotel. There was a Thai restaurant right across the street from them, and a little further down, a Tex-Mex restaurant.

"What are you in the mood for?" Tulia asked.

"I'm not sure. I kind of feel like we should get something Chicago's famous for — like pizza or hot dogs — but both are on the list of things the studio wants us to get footage of, so we might as well wait until tomorrow. Plus, I want something a little healthier."

"Let's keep walking, I'm sure we'll find something."

They walked to the end of the block and crossed the street. As they walked past a boutique pet store named Feather, Fur, and Fin, Tulia paused to peer through the windows. It was one of the nicest pet stores she had seen, and it looked like they had plenty of parrot supplies inside. The sign on the door said pets were welcome, so maybe she could bring Cicero there tomorrow and let him pick out some new toys.

"Ooh, donuts," Olivia said. Tulia tore her attention away from the pet store to see a cramped shop next to it with a neon sign in the window that simply read *Donuts*. The display case offered a tempting assortment of donuts and every other type of fried dough she could imagine, but as tempting as it looked, she knew she would regret eating so much food on an empty stomach.

The next shop was a used bookstore with a sitting area and a sign that said they served coffee and lattes. She wondered if it was connected to the donut shop or if they were completely separate businesses. Either way, she definitely wanted to visit both places before they left. The Book Nook was maybe not the most original name for a bookstore, but it made her think of the cozy window nook in their suite. They wouldn't have much downtime that week, but she was sure she would be able find an hour or two to curl up by the window and read.

The incessant gnawing of her stomach made her move on. There was so much to see and so much she wanted to do. She felt more like a tourist than she had for a long time, and almost wished she and Samuel could live somewhere like this for a year or two, but the blaring of a car horn from a few blocks over and the distant sound of sirens served to remind her that while Chicago had its shiny attractions, there were plenty of negatives to living in a major city as well.

A man in dirty clothes with a ratty blanket sat with his back against the brick wall at the end of the block. Tulia felt a pang of sympathy as they approached him. Loon Bay might not have much in the way of restaurants, but it didn't have a homeless population either.

"Hold on a second," she said to Olivia as she slowed down, reaching into her purse for her wallet.

Tulia didn't usually carry much cash on her, but she had stopped at an ATM the last time they got gas so she would have a way to tip the hotel employees. She took two twenties out of her wallet as they approached the homeless man. He didn't pay them any attention until she stopped and, feeling a little awkward, held the bills out to him, not sure what to say. He looked at her uncertainly then slowly took the twenties from her hand.

It was her turn to hesitate when he gestured at her to move closer. Wondering if he wanted to say something, she leaned down toward him. Faster than she could react, his hand darted out and plucked something off her shirt. When he pulled it back, she saw a dark gray feather pinched between his fingers.

"This came from an African Grey parrot, of the larger Congo variety," he said, squinting at it.

Tulia was surprised. The feather was gray, and not exactly attention grabbing. She wasn't sure if she would be able to tell it apart from a pigeon feather if she found one on the street.

"I own an African Grey, so it must have come from him," she told him. "How did you recognize it?"

"I used to be a zookeeper, if you can imagine that," he said gruffly. "I always liked working with the birds the best. I hope you take good care of him." He held the feather out to her.

"You can keep it," she told him. "Trust me, he leaves plenty of feathers for me. I have a big collection already. And I hope I'm taking good care of him. I do my best. My family's had him since I was born."

He tucked the feather into his pocket along with the money. She noticed he had an expensive looking camera around his neck, partially hidden by a scarf; it looked incongruously nice against the rest of his outfit. "I'm glad to hear that. Too many parrots spend their lives bouncing from home to home. They shouldn't be pets, not really. Most exotic animals shouldn't. It's a despicable trade."

Tulia wasn't sure how she felt about that. While she agreed that parrots weren't a pet for everyone, she truly did think Cicero was happy. Maybe he would have been happier in the wild, but he had been raised from an egg and domestically bred in the United States. There was no situation in which he would have had a chance to be a wild parrot, and as far as she knew, that was the case for most parrots these days.

She was well aware that the issue wasn't a straightforward one, however, and she was hardly going to get into an argument about it right now. "Well, it was nice to meet you. I'm Tulia by the way." She held out her hand, and he reached up to shake with her.

"Tommy," he said. "You keep taking care of that bird, you hear? If we keep something in a cage, we have responsibility to give it the best life we can, despite the bars."

He leaned his head back against the bricks and closed his eyes. Tulia started walking again, Olivia hurrying to catch up after spending another moment staring at him. They walked past an alley with an overflowing dumpster in it and continued on to the next block.

"I feel so bad for him," Olivia whispered. "Do you think he really lives on the streets? Why isn't he in a shelter?"

Olivia was young, in her early twenties, and much like Tulia, she hadn't had much experience with homeless people before leaving her hometown. Tulia had been all over the United States already and had seen and met people from all demographics, from those who were far wealthier than she was, to those who had less than nothing.

"There usually aren't enough shelters for everyone," Tulia told her quietly. "Or they have rules that the people who need to stay in them can't follow, like not allowing pets or an early curfew that might be impossible to make if someone works a job that keeps them late. It could also be that he just doesn't want to stay in one."

Olivia glanced over her shoulder, clearly discomfited. Tulia felt bad for him too, but what could they do? Maybe she could get him a hotel room for the night or find an ATM to take more money out for him, but she thought it might be better to ask him what he wanted first.

Maybe if he was still there when they were on their way back to the hotel, she could see if there was something they could do for him. For now, she nudged Olivia and nodded at a sandwich shop a little way further down the block and across the street. "That place looks good," she said. "What do you think?"

"Sure," Olivia said, brightening. "I hope they use fresh ingredients. I'm excited to eat something that doesn't come out of a can."

CHAPTER THREE

The sandwich shop turned out to be a good choice. Tulia got a club sandwich on whole grain bread with a side of hot, seasoned fries right out of the fryer. Olivia opted for a sandwich with cold cut turkey breast, provolone cheese, tomatoes, and a lot of bean sprouts. The food hit the spot for both of them. It wasn't as heavy as most of what they would end up eating for the rest of the week, and it had been a while since she'd had really good, quality bread. It made her want to get into baking, but she didn't exactly have room for a bread maker in her RV.

As they ate, they talked about what they wanted to do for the rest of the week. They would need time to film at each place they visited, and factoring in travel time meant they would probably only be able to go to two or three locations each day. It would be busy, but Tulia was looking forward to everything on their to-do list. She wanted to do at least one thing a day that Cicero could join them for, so he wasn't left alone in the hotel room for hours on end.

Thinking of Cicero made her remember Tommy, and before they left, she ordered another club sandwich for him, to go. It wasn't much, but it was something, and a good meal was something anyone could appreciate.

It was getting dark out by the time they left the restaurant. They crossed the street and started heading back up the sidewalk toward the hotel. There must have been a bar or a club further down, because Tulia could hear pounding music, and from the direction of the lake came the long, low sound of a horn—probably a barge. Everything felt so lively. She couldn't get over how much was going on; and to think this was only one tiny part of the city. It was hard to truly fathom how many people lived here.

Tulia had felt out of sorts since Samuel flew home after visiting her in Indiana, but now that they had gotten settled in their suite and she had a good meal in her stomach, and they had some solid plans about how to tackle the upcoming week, she was beginning to feel more like herself and once again excited for the rest of her adventure. Leaving her home behind was hard, but she had to remember it wasn't forever. It was a couple of months to do something she had been wanting to do anyway—finish seeing all fifty states. Samuel and the rest of her life in Loon Bay would be waiting for her when she got back.

"I don't think he's still there, Tulia," Olivia said as they made their way down the sidewalk and drew closer to the corner of the building where Tommy had been sitting.

"I see his blanket," Tulia said. "He must be nearby."

The sandwich in the to-go box felt too light as she clutched it in her hands. She wanted to do more to help him, but there were thousands of people just like him, and she couldn't help them all. How to give back to society and improve the lives of those who had less than she had was something she had wrestled with ever since she won the lottery. She didn't know if there was a perfect solution, but she tried to be kind and giving when she could.

The sandwich might not be much, but at least it was something, and she wanted to give it to him. She was sure Tommy was still around. They hadn't been in the restaurant that long, and his blanket and backpack were both still in the spot he'd been sitting in. She slowed her steps as they drew near the alley with the dumpster in it, and peered into the shadows, wondering if he had gone back there for some reason. The alley cut between the buildings and ended in a T where it met with an access street which she guessed was used for deliveries by the businesses in these buildings.

She didn't want to go in the dark alley, not unless she had to. She had just given Tommy forty bucks, so maybe he had gone to spend it somewhere. The donut shop? With Olivia following her, she continued past the alley and down the sidewalk, glancing into the bookstore as they passed it, and then stopping to look through the donut shop window.

She saw, to her disappointment, that it had closed for the evening while they were eating dinner. The display racks had been moved away from the window, and the lights inside were turned off. She really wanted one of those donuts, but maybe they would have time to get one tomorrow.

Turning around to suggest to Olivia that they leave the to-go box with Tommy's other things; she froze when she heard the sharp crack of a gunshot. The two of them stood there motionlessly as they listened, but no other shots rang out.

"Maybe someone's car backfired," Olivia suggested uncertainly. She looked nervous.

Tulia shook her head. "I don't think so. I'm almost certain that came from a gun."

It wasn't the first time she'd heard a gunshot and probably wouldn't be the last. Samuel owned a firearm for self-defense, and she had gone to the range with him a few times to make sure she knew how to use it, too. Many of his cases could be dangerous, and not just the homicides he investigated. Some people were willing to kill to keep their secrets, even if that secret was something as simple as an affair.

She had also heard gunshots in other, less savory situations than going to the range with her husband, and her gut told her this was one of those. They weren't in the middle of the countryside where someone might be shooting vermin or target practicing in their backyard. They were in the middle of a city, and there was no good reason for someone to be shooting on the city streets.

"It sounded like it came from close by," Olivia said, dropping her voice to a whisper.

Tulia's stomach twisted in unease. She wasn't sure what to do. Call the police? They couldn't have been the only ones who heard the noise, but she didn't know if anyone else would do it.

A faint sound from the alley they had just passed by —a groan and a clattering noise—made the decision for her. They had been in the middle of looking for Tommy, and they couldn't just give up on that. And that groan had sounded pained.

"We should go see what that was," she said, hoping she sounded braver than she felt.

Olivia, who had jumped and turned around at the noise, looked over her shoulder at Tulia doubtfully. "We just heard a gunshot and a mysterious sound in an alleyway, and you want to go see what it was?"

"It could be Tommy," she pointed out. "He couldn't have gone far, and like you said, that gunshot sounded close. He could be hurt."

"Whoever shot the gun might still be nearby," Olivia retorted. "I want to help people as much as you do, but I don't want to die."

Tulia hesitated because Olivia did have a point. There was a difference between doing what was right and trying to help someone and putting themselves in danger recklessly. She made her decision when she heard another clattering sound from the alley and shoved the sandwich box into Olivia's arms.

"I have to at least look," she said quietly. "If someone's hurt and we just walk away without even checking, I wouldn't be able to forgive myself."

Olivia accepted the sandwich box and began rummaging in her purse for her phone, a resigned look on her face. Tulia took her own phone out of her purse and dialed 911 with her finger poised over the call button. She began moving closer to the alley, slowly. The street was oddly quiet, though just a block down she could hear the steady rush of traffic traveling along the road that bordered the lake. She tried to reassure herself that help was close by, but could she really expect much help from complete strangers in a big city?

Trying to ignore the rapid pounding of her heart, she passed by the bookstore and approached the corner of the building where Tommy's belongings were. Careful not to step on his blanket or kick his bag, she pressed herself to the wall and crept closer, leaning forward to peer around the corner.

It took a second for her eyes to adjust. The narrow space between the buildings was dark with shadows, and it was hard to make anything out around the overflowing dumpster and piles of trash behind it. But then, something moved. Something big.

Her breath caught in her chest as she watched the shadows move. When the shape finally resolved and she realized what she was seeing, she became breathless for another reason. A person was dragging themselves down the alley—she was almost certain it was Tommy—moving painfully slow. With a sudden motion, the figure collapsed and didn't move again.

Tulia forced herself to scan the alley for another moment to see if anyone else was lingering in the shadows. When she didn't see anyone, she rushed forward, forgoing the 911 call in favor of turning on her phone's flashlight.

She was right. It was Tommy. He lay motionless on his stomach and without thinking, Tulia dropped to her knees to try to help him. Then she saw the sodden patch of dark red on his back, soaking into his clothing, and she froze.

The gunshot: it *had* been close by, and the victim was Tommy.

CHAPTER FOUR

At the sound of an empty can skittering across the pavement, Tulia jolted and looked up, her eyes fixing on a shadowed figure standing at the end of the alley where it met the access street in a T. She didn't have a chance to see any details; as soon as the person spotted her, they turned and fled to the right. Tulia stood up and ran past Tommy to the end of the alley. Before she reached the corner, she heard the slam of a heavy door, and when she finally turned onto the service road, it was empty and silent.

Whoever that person was, they must have escaped through one of the employee entrances behind the businesses on the access street. Breathing heavily, Tulia turned and hurried back to Tommy, shakily navigating back to the dial pad on her phone so she could hit the button to call 911. While the call rang through to the dispatcher, she carefully felt for his pulse, but she couldn't find it.

She spotted Olivia's nervous form at the mouth of the alley just as the dispatcher answered. Shaken, she stumbled over herself trying to tell the dispatcher what had happened. Thankfully, she knew the street the hotel was on, and Olivia agreed to stand at the entrance to the alley and wave the paramedics over when they arrived. As soon as the dispatcher had their location, the focus shifted to Tommy and trying to help him if she could.

Following the dispatcher's instructions, she carefully turned him onto his back and paused when she saw even more blood on the front of his shirt. Someone had shot him, though she couldn't tell if he had been shot in the chest or the back. Even as she tried to begin CPR, she knew in her heart it was too late.

Tommy was dead. No, he wasn't just dead—he had been *murdered.*

It seemed to take forever for the paramedics and the police to arrive, but once they did, everything passed by in a blur of flashing lights and sirens and brusque professionals that took over. The alleyway was cordoned off, and Tulia stood huddled with Olivia near the entrance, listening to the crackling of police radios as they watched the bustling response.

The detective who ended up speaking with them looked weary. It was strange to think that this was just another tragedy to him, one of hundreds he must have seen over his career, when Tommy's murder felt monumental to her. He took down their information, then began asking them rote questions. Tulia was glad she was able to give him Tommy's first name, even if she didn't know his last name or any information about him other than that he had been a zookeeper. It wasn't much to go on, but hopefully, it would help them track down his next of kin, if he had any.

She wished she had more to give them, but all she could offer was the brief conversation they'd had with Tommy on their way to the restaurant and the approximate time they'd heard the gun go off.

And one more thing; the sound of a slamming door and the empty alley after the mysterious figure fled the scene.

"That person has to be the one who shot him," she said when the detective didn't look as intrigued by this information as she had hoped. "And if they entered through an employee entrance in the alley, they must have had keys to whatever shop they went into, or at least knew the door would be unlocked, which means they have to work at one of these businesses, right?"

The detective sighed. "It's a possibility, but it's more likely that whoever you saw and heard was simply one of the shopkeepers checking on the commotion. No, this sort of crime is usually the work of gangs. Theft between members of the homeless population is common as well."

"But no one took anything from him," Tulia said. "His belongings are still right there on the sidewalk." She frowned. "I gave him forty dollars earlier. Is it missing?"

The detective called out to one of the officers, who went to search Tommy's pockets. A moment later, he poked his head out of the alley and held up two twenty-dollar bills. Tulia gave the detective a pointed look, but he simply shrugged.

"The killer got interrupted before they could search his pockets," he said. "I don't want you lovely ladies to worry about this. Enjoy your vacation. We'll canvass the neighborhood and see if anyone witnessed anything. Thank you for calling this in."

"Wait, what about his camera?"

The officer waved his coworker over and they whispered together for a moment before he shook his head. "No camera. You're free to go now. Take care."

Just like that, they were dismissed. Olivia, who seemed more shaken than angry, fell into step beside her as they began walking back up the block toward the hotel. It was completely dark out by now, and she kept her head on a swivel, her eyes wide as she peered into the shadows.

Tulia tried to let go of some of her frustration in order to focus on her friend. Olivia was frightened. Of course she was. She was in an unfamiliar city, and they had just witnessed a man get murdered. Tulia's frustration and sense of injustice could wait.

"How are you holding up?" she asked her friend as they drew near the hotel.

They didn't have key cards; rather, there was an app for their phones that they could scan to gain access to the building. Tulia pulled it up and held her cell phone out to the scanner to unlock the door while the younger woman formulated her response.

"I can't stop thinking about how close we came to coming face-to-face with whoever shot that poor man," Olivia said as they entered the building. "It could have been us. It could have been us, so easily."

Tulia was trying not to think about that. She knew going to check on the noises in the alley had been reckless, but she didn't know what else she could have done. Was it right to ignore someone who needed help just because there might be a danger to her? It would be different if the killer was with Tommy, but the alley had been empty of everyone except him when she checked it, and thankfully, whoever that other person was had fled when they saw her.

But if that person hadn't fled, and if they were the killer, then it was very possible the police would have responded to two murders tonight—one of them hers.

She took a deep breath. "But it wasn't," she said. "It wasn't us. We're all right. And look, we're back in the hotel. Completely safe for the rest of the night."

"Yeah," Olivia muttered. "I know we have a lot to be grateful for. I just can't stop hearing that gunshot over and over. I don't know how I'm going to get through the rest of this week and do all the filming that needs to be done for the documentary while I'm processing this."

"Let's see how you feel in the morning. If you need to, we can take a couple days off," Tulia said. "If your boss has a problem with it, he can talk to me."

The younger woman gave her a grateful look as they got into the elevator. Tulia hit the button for the tenth floor, and the elevator took them up. She realized her friend was still holding the to-go box with Tommy's sandwich in it and gently took it back from her. She wasn't sure what to do with it. It didn't feel right just to throw it away, but she wasn't sure if she would be able to eat it either. She decided to put it in the fridge and figure it out later.

When they reached their suite, she scanned her phone again to unlock the door. She was glad she had left one of the lights on in the living room because she knew Cicero got scared of the dark sometimes when they were in new places. They hadn't been planning on being gone for quite so long, and he let out a sharp whistle when he saw them enter the room.

"Hey, buddy," Tulia said.

She paused to engage both locks on the suite door and take her shoes off before putting the to-go box with Tommy's sandwich in the fridge. Olivia wandered over to the couch and flopped down on it, staring blankly out through the balcony window. It was a gorgeous view; the water and sky were dark except for the slowly moving lights from the boats and barges.

Tulia opened Cicero's cage and carried him over to the window nook to set him down on his towel so he could look out over the dark lake. She found the container of unsalted nuts she had put in the cupboard and brought him half of a walnut before sitting on the opposite end of the couch from Olivia.

Neither of them spoke. There wasn't much to say. Tulia felt emotionally exhausted, wrung out, and numb. She had witnessed a man's death today.

What was there to say about that?

CHAPTER FIVE

Before long, Olivia went into her own bedroom, and Tulia got up to chop some fresh fruits and vegetables for Cicero. Carrying his travel cage into her bedroom, she put his food bowl back in his cage and set him on his favorite perch, pausing to scratch the soft feathers of his head before she shut and latched his cage door. He sidled along the perch, the familiar sound of his claws against the wood comforting. She watched as he reached for a small cube of cucumber and gave him a fond smile before she turned away to get her pajamas out of the top drawer of the dresser.

The familiar routine of putting her hair in a bun to keep it dry and then hopping in the shower to rinse off before moisturizing and getting her pajamas on helped settle her thoughts. It was impossible not to feel a personal connection to Tommy and what had happened to him. Not only had she spoken with him less than an hour before his death, but she had witnessed the last moments of his life.

A part of her knew that the logical, smart thing to do would be to move on, to trust that the police would do the best they could and focus on her own job. But Chicago was a big city, and there were bound to be a lot of homicides; many of which would be easier to solve than Tommy's. The murder of a homeless man in a dark alley with no security cameras and no witnesses didn't leave much for the police to do. She was afraid Tommy's murder would become just another statistic, a cold case that would never get solved.

Even if she wanted to help, there might not be anything she could do. She still thought the fact that the person she'd seen at the end of the alley had fled through one of the employee entrances of the businesses that lined the access street was significant. She had been planning to go to the pet store, the donut shop, and the bookstore in the morning anyway, so maybe she could do some poking around. As long as she was careful, it couldn't hurt.

Unless she was right, and the killer was an employee or owner of one of the businesses. If they recognized her and realized what she was doing, she might end up in their crosshairs.

With a groan, Tulia flopped down on her bed. It was an astonishingly soft mattress that felt like she was getting a hug from a cloud. It only made her feel a little better. She knew what would help: a call with her husband. She needed to tell Samuel about what was going on anyway, and as much as he worried about her when she struck off on an investigation on her own, she knew he would understand why she felt like she couldn't let this go.

Sitting back up, she found her laptop where she had tucked it in the nightstand drawer and propped open the screen. It was a little later in Massachusetts than it was in Illinois, but she thought Samuel would still be up. They hadn't sent their goodnight texts yet, and he always waited for her to send one before going to bed. Thinking of how she would break the news to him, she selected his picture and started the video call.

Speaking with Samuel cleared her mind. He listened with an expression that grew ever more worried while she told him about meeting Tommy, buying the sandwich for him, and going back to find him only to hear the gunshot and discover that Tommy was the victim. He leaned forward, intrigued, as she told him about the mysterious figure who ran away and fled into one of the businesses' employee entrances, and he gave a sympathetic grimace when she shared her worry that Tommy's case would go unsolved among all the other crimes that took place in Chicago on a daily basis.

When she told him about her plan to go down to the shops the next day and ask some subtle questions about Tommy and the gunshot, he looked worried but resigned.

"Is Olivia going to help you?" he asked when she was done.

"I'm not sure," Tulia said. "She's pretty upset. She didn't sign up for this, and I don't blame her at all for how she's feeling. I don't want to ask her to do something she isn't comfortable with."

"Even if she isn't interested in helping you dig into what happened to Tommy, I think it would be a good idea if you kept her in the loop," he said. "That way you'll have backup, even if it's just someone who can call 911 if something goes wrong."

She could tell by the concerned look in his eyes and the set of his jaw that he was worried about her, but she knew he wouldn't try to convince her not to do this. He didn't have a leg to stand on, not when he investigated things like this for a living.

"I will," she assured him. "I'll be careful, Samuel. I just want to ask some questions, see if one of the locals knows more about Tommy or saw anything last night. I know the police are investigating, but I'm worried his case is going to slip through the cracks."

"Keep me updated," he told her. "Let me know if there's anything I can do to help. You didn't get his last name?"

"No, just his first name, and that he used to be a zookeeper. It's not much to go on, I know. Do you think you'd be able to help me track down his next of kin?"

"I can try," Samuel said, though he looked doubtful. "If you can learn anything else about him, it would help."

She promised to share whatever information she found with him, then the topic moved to other things —how things were going in Loon Bay, how work was going for him and Marc, how Rose, Tulia's goddaughter, was faring. She was only two years old, and Tulia felt like she was missing out on so much.

Her homesickness probably would have been worse if she wasn't so busy, but as it was, she had a very full week ahead of her and an important personal project on her plate now that she wanted to figure out who Tommy was and why someone had murdered him. She also had a city to explore. She didn't want to forget what she loved about traveling, and she wanted to take the time to enjoy Chicago and the rest of Illinois while she was here without thinking about the documentary or Tommy's murder.

There was a lot to keep her occupied, leaving only the quiet evenings for her to feel the full depth of how much she missed home and her husband.

Despite the soft mattress and soundproofed room, Tulia slept fitfully that night. She woke with the sun to the sound of Cicero whistling as dawn began to illuminate the room. When he saw her stir, he called out in Samuel's voice, "Hey! Whatcha doing? Want a snack?"

She sat up in bed and smiled at him, feeling groggy and unrested. "I just woke up, buddy, but I'll get you a snack in a second. You want a banana?"

He bobbed his head, then crouched on his perch and fluttered his wings to signify that he wanted to get out of his cage. She slipped off the bed and stretched, then walked over to fetch him, carrying him into the bathroom with her where he stood on top of the shower rod while she brushed her teeth and washed her face.

She felt bad about how boring yesterday had been for him. Thankfully, since she had gotten up so early, there was plenty of time before she and Olivia had to start working toward their goals for this part of the documentary. She got dressed, then carried him out into the living area, where she set him down on the towel she had placed in the reading nook so he could watch the world go by while she cut up part of a banana for him. She carried the fruit over on a saucer and set it down next to him, watching with a smile as he dug into his breakfast with gusto.

While he ate, she went back into her bedroom to organize her things and figure out what she wanted to bring with her today. She had a small backpack in which she kept the basics for a day out; a couple water bottles, some snacks, some emergency supplies, a little extra cash, and some sanitizing wipes. She had another bag with Cicero's things, including his harness and the elastic leash she used to take him outside.

As much as she would like to spend the whole day out with him, she couldn't take him with them today. They were planning on going to a restaurant for lunch and seeing a few museums in the afternoon. Later in the week, they would schedule a day to enjoy outdoor activities, and he would be able to tag along then.

But there was somewhere she could take him: the pet store. It was a short walk from the hotel, and pets were welcome inside. It would be a good chance for him to get out and about and see the city, and she could buy him some treats and toys while she was there. Plus, it would give her an excuse to talk to the employees at the pet store and see if any of them knew something about Tommy.

A quick search on her phone told her the pet store didn't open until eight, so she had a little time to tidy up the suite, not that it needed it, and drink some tea out on the balcony as she looked out over the lake. It was a beautiful late summer morning, the sort that promised a gorgeous, if hot, day to come.

At eight o'clock, she went back inside and got ready to go. After putting Cicero's harness on him, she sent a text to Olivia to let her know she was going down to the pet store but would be back within the hour.

To her surprise, the younger woman opened her bedroom door as Tulia was leaving and said, "Wait up a second, I want to come with you."

Tulia had thought Olivia would want to avoid the area around the pet shop, and any reminders of what happened to Tommy, but she didn't voice her surprise. Instead, she waited while Olivia ducked back into her bedroom to get dressed, then hurried out to grab her shoes and purse. They left the suite together, walking toward the elevator with Cicero perched on Tulia's hand. He looked around curiously as they got into the elevator and seemed unconcerned when it started to move.

Once they left the building, Tulia paused and leaned against the bricks to give Cicero a chance to get used to the noise, the wind, and the hustle and bustle of the city around them. It was a weekday, and rush hour was just starting, so the traffic was much worse than it

PATTI BENNING

had been the night before. She waited until Cicero relaxed enough to preen one of his flight feathers, then began striding down the sidewalk toward the pet store. Olivia walked beside her, taking in her surroundings as carefully as Cicero was.

"I'm glad we're not trying to drive in this," she muttered, glancing behind them at the lakeside road where traffic had slowed to a crawl. "If we do have to drive somewhere, we should make sure it's not during rush hour."

"Yeah, there's no sense in getting stuck in a traffic jam if we can avoid it," Tulia said.

She looked up at the buildings that towered above her. Walking through the city was a very different experience from walking along natural paths or through a small town, and it had filled her with a sense of adventure that even Tommy's murder couldn't completely dampen.

They crossed to the next block and reached the door of Feather, Fur, and Fin. A neon *Open* sign blinked at them. Tulia checked the signage on the door again to double-check that pets were allowed, but she had read it right the evening before. There was even a little

46

silhouette of a parrot with a leash along with other animals.

Looking forward to seeing what was inside, she pulled the door open and entered, pausing to hold it for Olivia before she turned around and took the store in.

CHAPTER SIX

She had been in plenty of pet stores in her life, but she knew right away this one was something special. There was a huge fish tank in the center of the store that she could hardly wait to get a closer look at. One wall was completely covered with toys and food and accessories for parrots and other birds. The other sections were marked by what sort of animal they were for. The pet shop seemed to cater to anything and everything someone who lived in a city could feasibly own; she saw sections for dogs, cats, rodents, birds, fish, and even a section simply marked exotic pets.

"We hit the jackpot," she murmured to Cicero. He looked a little nervous about his new surroundings, but when something screeched from the back of the store, those nerves turned into interest, and he responded with a piercing whistle.

The screech had come from a parrot, though the store must keep them in another room, since Tulia couldn't see any birds out on the main sales floor. That made sense; they allowed other people to bring pets, including pet birds, in and they would want to keep their own parrots safe from communicable diseases.

"Geez, seeing this place almost makes me wish I had a pet," Olivia said, looking around. "There's so much stuff. I'm going to go look at the fish tank."

The fish tank was the store's main attraction. It was circular, at least ten feet across and just as tall. As she drew closer and saw the coral and brightly colored fish inside, she realized it was a saltwater tank. It must have held hundreds of gallons of water, and she couldn't even imagine the amount of upkeep it needed. The end result was worth it, though. It was a little slice of the ocean in the middle of the city. She was pretty sure she even saw a miniature shark swimming around inside.

"I feel like I'm at the aquarium, but it's even better because it's free," Olivia murmured. "Oh, that reminds me. I got an email from my boss after I went to bed last night. He said he's trying to figure out how to get permission for us to film at Shedd Aquarium. I've always wanted to visit it, so I'd like to go either way."

"We'll add it to the list," Tulia said, unable to take her eyes off of the crystal-clear water and alien-looking critters in the tank. She had heard of Shedd Aquarium but had never been. "I want to go too."

Cicero leaned forward to tap his beak against the tank. She gently moved him further back, vaguely remembering hearing that you weren't supposed to tap on fish tanks because it bothered the fish. It seemed like Olivia was content to keep looking at the huge fish tank, which made sense considering that she didn't have any animals of her own to shop for, so Tulia headed toward the bird section with Cicero.

The sheer number of options was almost overwhelming. She did most of her shopping for him online since the majority of pet stores had a tiny bird section, if they offered anything for parrots at all. She was tempted to go overboard and buy him enough new toys to last him all year, but she had to remind herself that she had limited space in her RV, and she didn't even have her RV with her at the moment — it was currently in a long-term parking lot just outside of the city. She would have to keep her purchases to only a few things and resist the temptation to spoil her bird rotten.

"What do you think?" she murmured to her parrot. "Does anything catch your eye?"

Cicero was usually a little nervous around new toys, especially if they were a design or material he wasn't familiar with, but she saw him eyeing a toy made out of woven seagrass with chunks of bird-safe wood and bark tied onto it. The mat was folded over on itself and stuffed with shredded paper. It was a messy toy and one he would love to destroy. She grabbed it, then went to find a basket, and kept browsing.

"Hi, welcome to Feather, Fur, and Fin," a cheerful voice called out from behind her a few minutes later. "Can I help you find anything?"

Tulia's basket was already overflowing, but she didn't dare go back to get a cart from near the entrance. She knew there would be no end to her purchasing spree if she did. She turned around to see the woman who had spoken to her. She looked to be about Tulia's age, with dark blonde hair pulled back into a short pony-tail, a shirt with the pet store's logo on it, and a friendly smile. Her blue eyes were fixed on Cicero, and she was giving him an admiring look.

"I think I found everything I need," Tulia said. She had tossed a few bags of treats in there as well, for good measure. The basket was getting heavy, and she was glad she didn't have far to walk back to the hotel. "In fact, I'd better check out now before I overdo it."

The woman chuckled. She had a name tag that read *Store Owner*, and underneath that, her name, *Hannah*. "If you want to look around some more, you're welcome to leave your basket by the counter," she said. "You have a gorgeous bird, by the way. What's his name?"

"He's Cicero," Tulia said.

"Well, it's very nice to meet you, Cicero," she said, smiling at him. "We do have parrots and some other animals for sale in the back. You're welcome to take a look, but you won't be able to bring your bird back there with you. It's for the safety of both our own animals and our customers."

"I do want to look at them," Tulia said, biting her lip. She glanced at Olivia, who was still admiring the fish tank. "Would it be all right if my friend held him for me?"

"Of course. Come drop your basket off by the counter, and I'll show you where the hand sanitizer is. Since you have a parrot of your own, I'm sure you know this already, but I have to warn you not to stick your fingers in any cages, or you might lose them."

Olivia agreed to watch Cicero, who seemed almost as interested in the fish tank as she was. Tulia dropped her basket of parrot toys and treats off by the front counter and scrubbed her hands with hand sanitizer as she followed Hannah to the back of the store, where she opened a gate and gestured Tulia through.

Tulia stepped into a room that was even more stunning than the main sales floor. She had never seen so many parrots in one place before. She recognized cockatoos and amazons, macaws and conures. A caique was playing on a tree stand in the middle of the room, hopping from branch to branch and occasionally attacking a bell. In a huge stainless steel cage against the far wall, an enormous, dark blue hyacinth macaw clung to the bars and stared out at her.

The cages were all clean, with fresh water and food, but they seemed barren to Tulia. Each cage had only one toy in it, and one perch, and was just big enough to meet the minimum cage requirements for each species. She tried to reassure herself that the birds were only here temporarily before they went to new homes, but she still felt sad when she compared what they had to what Cicero's setup at home was like.

"We have a few greys over in the corner," Hannah said, pointing. "You can go talk to them if you want. They're both around six months old and we're trying to encourage them to pick up a few words."

Tulia walked past the cages, careful not to get close enough for any of the birds to reach out and grab her with sharp claws or beaks and found two cages in the corner that held a very familiar species.

One of the cages had a Congo African Grey, which was the same subspecies as Cicero. Even though both birds looked nominally the same, with light gray body feathers, darker grey flight feathers, and a bright red tail with a black beak, she knew that she would be able to tell the difference between this bird and Cicero in a heartbeat. The other cage held a Timneh African Grey, which was the smaller and darker of the two subspecies. About two-thirds of Cicero's size, the Timneh had dark gray feathers that were almost black in some areas, and a maroon tail. Both of the young birds climbed over to the bars to gaze out at her with friendly, curious expressions.

Her heart melted. She couldn't remember what Cicero was like when he was this young, since she had been a six-month-old baby herself, and it made her wish she remembered more of his adolescent years. "Look at you two cuties," she crooned. "You're going to find great homes; I just know it. They'll love you every bit as much as I love Cicero."

After chatting with the greys for a few moments, she walked over to the hyacinth macaw, which was the most eye-catching bird in the room. She had looked them up before out of curiosity and knew their care requirements were demanding, and they had a price tag to match, starting at twenty thousand dollars on the low end.

She might be able to afford that price, but she didn't think she would be able to give a bird this size the care it needed, especially not since she would be sharing her attention with Cicero. That didn't mean she couldn't look, though. He was an absolutely gorgeous bird, covered all over in dark blue feathers. The skin around his huge, curved beak was bright yellow, as was the ring of skin around his dark eyes.

"You are absolutely gorgeous," she said. He made a quiet honking sound in response.

"Do you want to hold him?" Hannah asked.

Tulia turned around; her eyes wide. "No, I couldn't. I'm just looking. I'm not going to buy another bird. Cicero is more than enough for me."

"That's all right," Hannah said. "He's less than a year old, and we're trying to make sure he stays well socialized until someone buys him. I always prefer letting someone who already owns parrots hold him, since you know what you're doing. He's very friendly, but you don't have to if you don't want to."

"No, I do," Tulia said quickly.

Hannah grinned at her, and Tulia stepped back as she opened the stainless steel cage. She stuck her arm in fearlessly, and the giant bird stepped up on it. He looked even bigger out of the cage, somehow. Usually, Cicero stepped up on her fingers, but there was no way a bird this size would be able to comfortably balance on her hand like that, so she held her whole arm out like Hannah had done.

"Step up," Hannah encouraged him.

The bird stepped onto her arm. His feet were so big that his claws reached almost all the way around her wrist, though thankfully they were trimmed and blunted, so they didn't scratch her. His scaly feet were warm, and she was very proud of herself for not flinching when he reached down to rub his beak on her arm.

A bite from a beak that size would mean a trip to the hospital.

"He likes it if you scratch the feathers on top of his head."

Tulia complied, raising her hand more hesitantly than she would have with Cicero. The big blue bird bowed his head, and she gently scratched the warm skin under his feathers.

"Wow," she breathed as Hannah took him back and returned him to his cage. "He's beautiful."

"He's going to make someone an amazing, lifelong companion," Hannah said. "Would you like to see some of our other exotics?"

"Sure," Tulia said, not sure what to expect as Hannah led her through to another room.

This one was a little smaller and without any windows, though she saw UV lights in each corner. There were two additional doors in this room. One was labeled as an exit and must have led out to the service street behind the building. The other door was unlabeled, but the three different locks installed on it caught her eye.

Hannah saw her looking at the door and said, "That's where we keep our sick or injured animals and incubating eggs," she explained. "We don't want any guests to wander back there accidentally."

"I see."

Tulia was soon distracted by the sight of all the other animals in this room. She was stunned, even more so than she was with the birds. Could all these animals really be legal to own in Chicago? There were monkeys — little marmosets the size of her hand and one cage that held a larger monkey in it, something she thought might be a capuchin. She saw sugar gliders and strange animals the size of cats with round, nocturnal eyes. A cage in the corner held a litter of spotted kittens.

"Ocelots," Hannah said proudly. "They make good house pets as long as you know what you're getting into. We offer care courses for all the animals we sell, of course."

Tulia, who had never seen monkeys in person other than at the zoo, wandered over to the cage with the marmosets in it. Like the birds, all the cages were clean but mostly barren. From behind the locked door, she heard a yipping sound.

"Wow," she said again, feeling a little stunned. "I don't think I've ever seen so many different animals in one place."

"We sell the greatest variety of exotics of any pet store in the state," Hannah said proudly. "I'll give you my business card. We're able to ship most of our species out of state, so if you see something you like now, you can always order it later."

Tulia took the business card to be polite, but she felt a little disconcerted at the sight of all the animals for sale. She owned a parrot, so she knew how popular exotic animals were, but seeing them being treated as commodities didn't sit right with her.

"You have an amazing store," she said as Hannah walked to the front counter with her. It was the truth. Tulia had never seen a store like it before. "I can't imagine how much work it must be to take care of all those animals, though."

"It's definitely not for the faint of heart," Hannah said as she began scanning Tulia's items. "I'm here all day, every day. I don't trust my employees to take care of the animals the same way I would, so I'm here even on the holidays."

"Were you here yesterday, then?" Tulia asked, trying to sound casual. "My friend and I were walking back from dinner when we saw a lot of police gathered in the alleyway next to this building. Do you know what happened?"

It wasn't a lie, exactly. She had just omitted a lot that had happened in between.

Hannah frowned. "A homeless man was found dead. It's not the sort of thing that happens in this area. Don't let it scare you away, though."

"Did you know the man at all?" Tulia asked.

Hannah shook her head. "I think the guy who owns the donut shop used to give him free food sometimes, but I never had much of a reason to interact with him. He didn't have a pet, and it's not like he was about to waltz in here and buy a thousand-dollar animal. I saw him on the corner sometimes, but that was about it."

Tulia handed her card over with a thoughtful frown. It sounded like whoever owned the donut shop might know more about Tommy than Hannah did.

"Thanks," she said, as Hannah handed her back her card and then the plastic bag with Cicero's things in it. "And thanks for showing me all the animals in the back. I enjoyed holding the hyacinth macaw. He really is gorgeous. I'd be tempted if I didn't have my hands full with Cicero."

"No problem," Hannah said with a smile. "And you know, having two birds isn't that much more work than one is. Your grey might like having a companion."

Tulia would be lying to herself if she said she wasn't a little tempted by the thought of bringing that gorgeous blue macaw home, but as she turned away and took Cicero back from Olivia, she knew she wouldn't be able to give them both the attention they deserved. Even when she was done with this road trip, she had a full life in Loon Bay to think about, and her future dreams of raising a family.

No, Cicero was enough for her.

CHAPTER SEVEN

Tulia told Olivia about the different animals she had seen as they left the pet store. She might have gone a little overboard with her presents for Cicero, but he would enjoy having a bunch of new toys to tear apart.

"I'd like to check out the donut shop and the bookstore too, though I should probably go back to the hotel first to drop off Cicero and his things," she said once they were out of the store.

"I can hold him while you go in," Olivia said. "I don't mind."

"Are you sure?"

Olivia nodded. "Just grab me a donut. I'm guessing you're going to ask questions about Tommy, and I'd rather not be involved. Plus, Cicero and I are buddies. Remember when we first met, and he gave me the stink eye all the time? I think he's finally starting to like me."

Even though Olivia had volunteered, Tulia still felt a little guilty as she left her friend, her bird, and Cicero's bag of parrot toys and treats on the sidewalk while she went into the donut shop. While the donut shop wasn't quite as impressive as the pet store had been, it certainly came close. The air smelled sweet and rich with the scent of sugar, vanilla, and buttery caramel, and the store offered the biggest variety of donuts and related treats, such as fritters, that Tulia had ever seen.

The shelves held everything from plain donuts to iced and filled monstrosities the size of a plate, the latter of which were true works of art. There were donuts with edible glitter and sprinkles, donuts with apple butter filling, maple glazed donuts with bacon crumbles on top, and so much more.

"Hi, there. I'm Derek, and you look like a lady who's in the mood for some sugar."

Tulia looked up at the man who came through a swinging door behind the counter. He was wearing an apron covered in cartoon donuts and had a hair net over his curly black hair. He had caught her staring at the glass display case by the counter, where she had been ogling a brownie fudge donut that looked like it contained more chocolate than she normally ate in a month.

"I thought I'd be able to run in and quickly grab something for my friend and myself," Tulia said, "but I don't even know where to start."

Derek glanced at the window, through which they could see Olivia and Cicero standing on the sidewalk. "A lot of people find it hard to decide," he assured her. "We're running a baker's dozen special right now —get a box of a dozen donuts and get the thirteenth for free, and I'm also happy to let you sample something if you have a question about the flavor. And have you been to The Book Nook next door? We have a partnership with them, where you'll get fifteen percent off your drink order if you have a receipt from here with the current date on it. You're welcome to eat in there, and even though they don't advertise it, they allow well-behaved pets to come in."

"Really?" Tulia glanced out the window at Cicero, who was letting Olivia pet him. They could get donuts and coffee and browse The Book Nook before they went back to the hotel. It sounded like the perfect way to spend the morning. "Thanks for letting me know. I guess I'll get a full dozen donuts. I'm not sure if we'll eat them all, but we can probably find people to share with."

"That's what I like to hear," the man said, as he got a paper box down from a shelf and folded it into the right shape. "I always encourage people to buy extra and share. I don't know if you saw the sign, but we donate our extra donuts to food banks and shelters and sell our day-old donuts for a dollar per half dozen to anyone who's on a government assistance program. If you're interested in learning more about our programs or donating, I can give you a business card with our website on it."

"Sure. It's great that you give back to the community." She remembered what Hannah had said about him giving free food to Tommy sometimes. It seemed in line with who he was so far. "Did you know the homeless man who used to stay on the corner of the block?"

His expression fell. "Tommy? Yeah, I knew him pretty well. He passed away yesterday. I'm still recovering from the news. He's been a regular here for a long time. He'd come around to the back to talk while I was taking the garbage out, and I always held back a few fresh donuts for when I saw him. It's tough to believe he's gone now."

"My friend and I met him not long before he died," Tulia said. "Do you know what happened to him?"

He frowned. "I'm not sure. The police spoke to me briefly, but they didn't give me any details. I was cleaning up in the kitchen after closing for the evening, and I always play music while I'm doing that, so if there was a struggle, I wouldn't have heard it. I'm still kicking myself for that. The police wouldn't be investigating so thoroughly if he had died from natural causes, which makes me think it must have been a violent crime. It makes me feel sick to think Tommy was attacked and killed while I was in here jamming to music and wiping down counters. I just hope it wasn't my fault."

Tulia couldn't keep her eyebrows from rising in surprise. "What do you mean?"

He hesitated. "I gave him a loan a couple of weeks ago, something I was hoping would help him get back on his feet. He was a good guy. My worry is he might have told the wrong person about it, and they decided to rob him, and that was what got him killed."

Tulia filed the information away. It was the first potential motive she'd heard. "Have you told the police about the loan?"

"I did," he said. "Not sure how much will come of it. Anyway, you're here to buy donuts, not talk about my problems. What do you have your eye on?"

Tulia walked along the shelves, picking the donuts that looked the most intriguing while he put them in the box for her. They returned to the counter, where she paid for the donuts and added a tip to his donation jar.

"I hope you enjoy them. It was nice to meet you…" He reached over the counter to shake her hand.

"Tulia," she said. "And thanks. I'm sure we will. These look amazing."

A dozen donuts might have been going overboard, but there were so many flavors she wanted to try. As she walked out of the store with her box of donuts in hand, she pondered over the little she knew about Tommy so far.

Was the loan from Derek, an act of kindness, the reason Tommy lost his life?

CHAPTER EIGHT

"I asked you to get me *a* donut," Olivia said, peering at the box. "I'm not sure the two of us can survive eating that much sugar by ourselves."

"I thought we could see if the bookstore has a plastic knife that we can use to cut them into pieces," Tulia said. "That way we can each try as many of the different types as we want, and we can find someone else to share the rest with."

"I'd like to go into the bookstore with you," Olivia said. "If we're going there next, would it be all right if we went back to the hotel with Cicero to drop him off first?"

"We can," Tulia said, "but according to Derek, the man who owns the donut shop, The Book Nook allows well-behaved pets inside. They also have some sort of partnership with the donut shop, and we'll get a discount with this." She held the receipt up.

Olivia raised her eyebrows. "Let's go, then. Here, do you want Cicero back? I can take the donuts."

They traded and walked the short distance to The Book Nook's door. Olivia pulled it open for her, and Tulia maneuvered herself, Cicero, and his bag of goods inside as the younger woman brought up the rear. The bookstore smelled like coffee and old paper, which was a winning combination, in Tulia's opinion. A middle-aged woman with long ginger hair was standing at the front counter, scanning a pile of books at the computer before carefully putting them into a cardboard box. She looked up when Tulia and Olivia came in and gave them a warm smile.

"Welcome to The Book Nook. Make yourselves at home. If those are donuts I see, you're welcome to enjoy them in here, but we ask that you keep all food and drink in the Nook Corner." She gave the bag from Feather, Fur, and Fin a sour look. "You can put your bag over there, too."

She nodded to a cozy corner by the windows with a couple of small tables, a couch, armchairs, and a coffee table. There were board games and a shelf of kids' books and toys against one wall.

"This is so cozy," Olivia said as they walked over to the Nook Corner to put the donuts down on the coffee table before returning to the front counter.

"Is this your first time here?" the woman asked.

"Yep. We're from out of town," Tulia explained. "We're staying at a hotel just up the street and wanted to explore the local area."

"Well, I'm glad you decided to stop in here," she said. "Your bird is adorable, by the way. You're welcome to walk around with him, but please keep him away from the books—I used to have a sun conure, and I know how much damage those beaks can do—and please clean up any messes right away. It's very nice to meet the two of you. I'm Miranda. Can I get you some coffee or tea to go with your donuts?"

They took a moment to peruse the menu that was written on a small chalkboard next to the computer. The menu was limited, but the options were all drinks that Tulia enjoyed, so it was hard to choose. In the end, she decided to get an iced caramel macchiato, while Olivia opted for a vanilla latte.

"Coming right up," Miranda said after they showed their receipt from the donut shop for their discount and paid for their drinks. "Mind if I ask what genres you enjoy reading?"

"I don't read all that much," Olivia admitted. "When I do, it's usually something light, like romance or young adult fiction. I used to read a lot more when I was younger, but I think I kind of burned out on it during college."

"I like mysteries," Tulia said. "I enjoy some historical fiction and nonfiction, too."

"Well, I've got just the thing for you, if you don't mind a bit of self-promotion," Miranda said, nodding at Tulia. "I'm a self-published author, and my specialty is mysteries. Not to toot my own horn, but my books have gotten great reviews so far. You can find all of my novels on that display, over there."

Tulia spotted a display with a sign that read *Miranda Lee, Local Author* on top of it. "I'll definitely check them out," she promised. "It's always exciting to find a new author I like."

They accepted their drinks and headed back over to the Nook Corner to open up the box of donuts. Tulia kept Cicero on her shoulder as she tucked his bag of items out of the way and tried to decide which donut she wanted, and Olivia jumped up to grab a plastic fork from Miranda so they could divide them into pieces.

Tulia chose to try that fudgy brownie donut she had been eyeing first, and she wasn't disappointed. It was dense and chocolatey and surprisingly not too sweet. Most of the flavor came from the chocolate itself rather than the sugar. She made a wordless noise of appreciation while Olivia chose a strawberry short-cake donut topped with real strawberries to try.

The coffee was good too, and the bitterness paired well with the sweetness of the donuts. It was clear that they weren't going to come anywhere near finishing the dozen donuts before they started getting stale, so they set aside their favorites and Tulia got up to ask Miranda if she'd like to keep the rest of the box of donuts to offer to her customers, but when she looked over at the counter, she saw that Miranda was gone, along with the box of books.

Since she was already up, she turned her attention to the books Miranda had written. With Cicero watching from his perch on her shoulder, she read the backs of the books and tried to decide which one she wanted to buy. It looked like they were all standalone novels instead of part of a series, which was nice. She hated it when a book ended on a cliffhanger, and she had to wait for the next one to come out.

When she spotted a title with a parrot on the front, she knew immediately that was the one she was going to choose. The parrot in question was an Amazon parrot, with yellow feathers on its head and green feathers on the rest of its body. The back blurb indicated that the book was about animal trafficking, so she hoped it wouldn't be too sad, but some of the featured reviews under the blurb promised that it was funny and well written, so her hopes were high.

"Sorry about that," Miranda said as she returned from the back of the bookstore. "I needed to get that package ready to go before our mailwoman shows up. We just finished setting up our online store, and the orders have been rolling in. It's been busy, but I'm just glad we're moving inventory. Everyone thinks they want to own a bookstore until they see how hard it is to stay out of the red."

"It must be tough to make a profit," Tulia said as she set the book down on the counter. "Most people buy their books online these days, don't they?"

Miranda nodded as she scanned the book. "Oh, this is a good one. It was a lot of fun to write. And you're right. Thankfully, there are still a lot of people who swear by physical books. I've been worried more than once that I'd have to close this place down, but fate seems to be on my side. Something always happens at the last minute that lets me keep it running for a little bit longer. Will you be paying with cash or card?"

Tulia handed her card over and idly reached a hand up to stroke Cicero's feathered head as Miranda rang her up. "Are you familiar with a homeless man named Tommy? He was sitting at the corner of the block right next to your bookstore yesterday."

Miranda's friendly expression closed off between one heartbeat and the next. "Tommy? I didn't know that was his name. I've seen him, of course, but never paid much attention to him. He didn't bother the customers, so I never had a reason to."

"Do you know anything about what happened to him?"

"I know there was some sort of commotion last night, but I wasn't aware it had anything to do with him. If he has a family, they have my thoughts and prayers, and I hope he's at peace now. Here's your book. I'd really appreciate it if you'd leave a review. Is there anything else I can help you with?"

Miranda seemed eager to get Tulia out of her hair, so Tulia simply thanked her, took the book, and headed back to the couch where Olivia was sitting. She had forgotten to ask about the donuts, but they could do that when they left.

As she sat down and slipped her book into the bag from the pet store so she wouldn't forget it, she glanced back at the counter where Miranda was studiously fixated on the computer. Something about the way the bookstore owner reacted to hearing about Tommy struck her as odd. She said she hadn't known what the commotion was about, so how had she known Tommy was dead? And why had she been in such a hurry to change the topic?

Frowning, Tulia turned her focus back to Olivia and picked up her coffee as they began to discuss where they wanted to go next. Maybe she was being paranoid. Chances were low that Miranda was involved in Tommy's death. After all, what motive could a bookstore owner possibly have to kill a homeless man?

CHAPTER NINE

Once they left the bookstore—sans donuts—Tulia called Samuel to give him a quick update while they walked back to the hotel. She gave him Hannah's, Derek's, and Miranda's names, along with the names of their stores, though she wasn't very optimistic that a background check would be all it took to blow the case open. She knew she needed to come to terms with the fact that she might not be able to help Tommy get the justice he deserved, but the stubborn part of her didn't want to give up just yet.

If he had been killed by a random act of violence from a complete stranger, then there wasn't much she could do. But she knew the statistics. Most homicides were committed by someone the victim knew, and since she was sure the person she had seen fleeing the scene the night before was the killer, and they had access to one of the employee entrance doors that lined the access road, then it stood to reason the killer was someone who owned or worked at one of the three stores she had just visited.

She knew she could be wrong, but she only had a limited amount of time in Chicago, and she had to focus on the most likely suspects first.

After returning to the hotel room to drop off Cicero and his bag of toys, Tulia and Olivia turned their focus to the tasks they had to complete for the studio this week. They needed some footage of the city, so they set out on foot for an area with some nicer stores and high-rise buildings. It was a hot day, and even though they were working, it felt a little like being on vacation. They paused to admire a row of townhouses with car turntables; a rotating circle of concrete that could turn a car around after it was parked. Olivia had never seen them before and was fascinated by the concept.

They wouldn't be able to explore all of the city on foot, but it was a nice day for walking. Tomorrow they could get her sedan out and explore some locations that were further away. For now, Tulia was just glad to be in a new state and getting back to their normal routine. It had been great seeing her parents and Samuel over the past few weeks, but it had thrown their schedule off and made her think about everything she was missing out on.

Exploring Chicago on foot with Olivia made her remember how much fun it was to visit new places, and why she had agreed to do this documentary in the first place.

For lunch, they stopped at a food truck that was selling smoothies next to a small park. The smoothies were good but were almost as sweet as the donuts. The sugar gave her a temporary boost of energy, but by the time dinner rolled around and they had been on their feet all day, they were both starving, which was perfect for their last filming location of the evening: the highest rated Chicago pizzeria they could find.

Tulia had never understood the animosity between fans of different types of pizza. As far as she was concerned, all pizza was good, whether it was deep dish or a New England thin crust or something in between. But she had never had a real Chicago deep dish pizza, and when they ordered a medium Chicago deep dish pizza to share at the pizzeria with the best reviews in the area, she realized she might have a new favorite.

As soon as she pulled the first cheesy slice away, she knew she was in for a treat, and the taste did not disappoint. With a deep pan-shaped crust and a thick layer of melty cheese topped with house-made marinara sauce, it was an indulgent meal. Considering how many calories she had burned walking around all day, she let herself enjoy it guilt free.

At first, she had been self-conscious of Olivia filming her while she was eating, but she had gotten used to it and trusted Olivia and the studio not to include any footage that was outright bad. They weren't out to embarrass her, after all. She was the star of the show, as weird as that was to think, and they would only let the best pieces of footage get through their editing process. Still, she was glad when Olivia finally put the camera down and started to eat her own food.

"I think that's it for today," the younger woman said as she picked up a slice of pizza, trying not to let the toppings fall off. "I feel good about the amount of filming we got done."

"Me too," Tulia said. "Do you want to go to the aquarium tomorrow?"

"I still haven't heard back from my boss about whether or not we have permission to film there, but I could always contact the aquarium myself and ask," Olivia said. "If we can't, we should probably keep it until our last day and make sure we have time to get everything else done first."

Tulia was looking forward to seeing the aquarium, but they did have a lot they still needed to do. Before she could agree, her phone began ringing. She fished it out of her purse and spotted Samuel's name on the caller ID.

"Do you mind if I get this?" she asked Olivia.

"Go ahead," Olivia said, taking her own phone out. "It gives me an excuse to scroll mindlessly online guilt free. I could use the brain break."

Tulia answered Samuel's call. They exchanged pleasantries and she told him what they had done all day. She promised to send him a picture of their pizza so he could live vicariously through her and asked him what he'd eaten for dinner—a tuna salad sandwich and a slice of rhubarb pie one of his clients had left at the office as thanks—then they got down to business.

"I ran the names through a basic background check," he told her. "Didn't come up with much, other than for Derek Simmons. He has a criminal record, including armed robbery, but it looks like he got his life straightened out after that."

"Hold on, armed robbery? Did he hurt anyone?"

"I didn't see any assault convictions, but you never know if a charge was dropped, or they reached a plea deal."

She frowned, thinking. If Derek had a felony, then he couldn't legally own a firearm, but she doubted that mattered much. Lots of people owned guns illegally. He had a criminal history, which included armed robbery, and he'd given Tommy a sizable loan that seemed to have vanished into thin air. Had he wanted the loan back and gotten angry when Tommy couldn't pay?

"Thanks, Samuel," she said. "No luck figuring out what Tommy's last name is or if he has any next of kin?"

"Unfortunately, no. Variations on the name Tom are common, and there isn't exactly a list of zookeepers I can cross-reference. Let me know if you get any other identifying information for him, and I'll keep looking."

Even the people who had seen Tommy every day didn't seem to know much about him, so learning enough to identify his family seemed like an impossible task, but Tulia was determined to do something for him. If she couldn't figure out who killed him, then the least she could do was track down his family and tell them what happened to him. Maybe they would be able to keep the case moving forward after she and Olivia left the state.

CHAPTER TEN

They made it back to the hotel before dark, and Olivia went straight into her bedroom to organize and label the footage and email it to her boss. She had gotten anxious as the light began to fade while they were walking back from the restaurant, and Tulia was starting to feel jumpy too by the time they reached the hotel. Tommy's death was an unwelcome reminder of how quickly an act of violence could change everything.

Left to her own devices, Tulia took Cicero out of his cage and turned on some music to give him something to listen to while she put their leftover pizza in the fridge. She wished she had kept some of the donuts from earlier, but she could always go get more in the morning.

Tomorrow would be another busy day, but for tonight they were done. She finally had time to relax, if she could manage it, but she couldn't stop thinking about Tommy. She wished she'd had Cicero with her when they spoke to him. He probably would have liked seeing the bird in person, and maybe it would have made his last hours a little happier.

Feeling morose and not wanting to distract herself with mindless TV shows—she saved her favorites to watch with Samuel whenever they had time to video chat for a couple hours—she grabbed the book she'd bought earlier and settled into the window reading nook with Cicero perched on one of her knees.

While he preened his feathers, she cracked the book open and began reading, skimming through the author's note. She was in the mood for a good mystery and hoped Miranda's writing would suck her in immediately. If she liked this one, then she would buy more of Miranda's books before they left.

She turned the page and skimmed over the acknowledgments next, already reaching for the next page as her eyes flicked over unfamiliar names, only to falter when she reached the very last one.

And a special thanks to Tommy Martin, whose years of experience as a zookeeper and animal welfare activist made this book possible.

There wasn't a picture, but her blood ran cold, none-theless. How many zookeepers named Tommy could Miranda know? She flicked back to an earlier page and checked the date the book had been printed. It had been published just a few months ago. She didn't know how long Tommy had been living in the area, but maybe Derek would. Was this him? Had Tommy collaborated with Miranda on her book?

She didn't know Tommy's last name, and Samuel was right that Tommy, Tom, and other variations of the name were common, but it was too much of a coinci-dence to ignore. She just didn't understand why Miranda would have lied about knowing him if she'd known him well enough to acknowledge him in her mystery novel.

She flipped the pages to the back of the book, careful to avoid spoilers, in hopes that there might be more acknowledgements in the back of the book, but she didn't find anything useful. The *About the Author* section featured a paragraph about Miranda's life and her bookstore, but there was no other information about Tommy or the people she consulted with for her books.

She wanted to know more. She wanted to know why Miranda acted like she didn't know Tommy, when here was his name in print, right in front of her face. She picked up her phone and searched the Book Nook online, but it was already closed. Her questions would have to wait until the morning.

The book was surprisingly good. It hooked her from the start, and she made it about a third of the way through before she went to bed for the night. She felt like she was missing something, some motivation for Miranda to lie about Tommy, but as she lay there in the darkness and tried to figure out what it could be, she couldn't come up with anything.

In the morning, she fed Cicero his breakfast and got dressed as soon as she woke up. Olivia was still in the shower by the time Tulia was ready to go, so she texted the other woman to let her know she was getting donuts and coffee and would be back soon. One elevator ride later, she found herself back on the sidewalk outside the hotel. Today was overcast and humid. True to the city's nickname, the wind had picked up, and as she started down the sidewalk, she wished she had a hair tie.

She crossed to the next block and slowed as she passed the pet store. It was tempting to go inside and see that beautiful hyacinth macaw again, but she already knew she wasn't going to adopt him, and she didn't want to waste Hannah's time. She continued on to the donut shop. This time, Derek was behind the counter when she entered.

"Welcome back," he said as she entered. "Where's your pet and your friend?"

"They got a slow start this morning," she said. "I'm only going to get two donuts this time, though I might be back later this week to get more."

"Got you hooked, huh?" he asked, grabbing a paper pastry bag. "What are you in the mood for?"

She pointed out a custard-filled glazed donut and strawberry shortcake one, remembering that Olivia had liked that one best the day before. While he rang her up, she decided to ask him a few questions.

"I was wondering, do you know how long Tommy had been living in the area?" she said.

Derek raised his eyebrows. "I've been seeing him regularly for about half a year, but I saw him around occasionally for a while before that. How come?"

"I'm just trying to learn more about him," she said. "My husband's a private investigator, so it's hard for me to ignore something like a homicide when it happens practically right in front of my face."

It was a risk, mentioning Samuel's career to someone who might be involved in the murder, but Derek didn't look worried or distrustful. If anything, his expression cleared.

"Well, I'm sure Tommy would appreciate it. I'm hoping the police will come up with a suspect soon, but having more people on the case won't hurt."

She paid for her donuts and accepted the bag from him. "Did you ever see Tommy and Miranda talking? I picked up one of her books yesterday and noticed she mentioned a Tommy Martin, who was a zookeeper and animal welfare activist, in the acknowledgments. That has to be him, right?"

"Yep, that's Tommy," Derek said, his expression turning sad. "He and Miranda would chat sometimes. During the colder months, she let him come in and read in her little Nook Corner until closing. That's how I met him, actually—I go over there for free coffee sometimes, and to see if I can convince Miranda to let me take her to dinner." He grinned. "No luck on the latter yet, but I think she's warming up. It's only been about three years."

Tulia chuckled. "Well, good luck with that. I'm more of a mystery reader myself, but it sounds like a love story that would make a great romance novel. And thanks for answering my questions about Tommy."

"Anytime," he said. "I wish I could do more to help. Heck, I wish I had done more to help him. Looking back, I think I could have done a lot more."

She said goodbye to Derek and left the donut shop, pausing to glare up at the sky when she felt some sprinkles on her face. "Give me fifteen minutes," she muttered to the clouds. "I should be back at the hotel by then."

She quickly walked the distance to the bookstore and slipped through the front door. Miranda wasn't at the counter, but an electronic bell over the door had gone off, so she was sure the other woman knew she was there. While she waited, she wandered back over to the display that featured Miranda's books and put her bag of donuts down so she could check the acknowl-edgments in the other books she had written for Tommy's name.

It looked like the book about animal trafficking was the only one she had consulted Tommy about, which made sense, considering his realm of expertise. After reading the blurbs, she decided to get another of Miranda's books, this one featuring a mystery that took place on a ferry on Lake Michigan. She picked her donuts back up and carried the book over to the front counter. Buying the book would give her a reason to talk to Miranda, and it would be a natural segue into mentioning seeing Tommy's name in the acknowledgments in the one she was currently reading.

She waited for a few minutes, gradually growing more restless as Miranda failed to appear. She looked around but didn't spot a bell to ring for service.

"Hello?" she called out. Her voice sounded too loud in the quiet bookstore. Miranda didn't answer.

Tulia wandered farther into the bookstore. There was a side room that she had seen Miranda go into yester-day, but the door was currently shut. She knocked on it, but there was no response, and when she tried the doorknob, it was locked.

"Miranda, are you in there? Or anyone else?" Nothing. The bookstore remained silent.

She turned away from the door and walked deeper into the bookstore, peering between the shelves. She was beginning to get worried. The back of the store housed the used books section, and it also looked like it was where Miranda kept her incoming and outgoing deliveries. Two tables were loaded high with boxes, and next to them was the employee entrance, which was propped open with a brick.

"Miranda?"

She approached the employee entrance and peeked out into the access street. Nothing to her left. She inched farther out so she could look around the door to the right. The street was empty. Before she could pull her head back inside, she saw the next door down open and Derek looked out. He spotted her immediately and gave her a look of surprise, his eyebrows crawling halfway up his forehead until they were almost hidden in his hairnet.

"What are you doing out here?" he asked.

"I'm looking for Miranda," Tulia said. "I wanted to buy another one of her books, but she isn't in the bookstore. No one's here, it's just me."

His eyes widened. "You're *sure* she isn't in there?"

"There's a locked door I can't get through, but I knocked on it and she didn't respond. I guess she could be on the other side, but I have no way of knowing."

"That's concerning," he said. "I thought I heard someone scream. That's why I'm out here; I wanted to make sure it didn't come from the access street. After what happened to Tommy, I didn't want to take any chances. But if Miranda's missing … what if it's her?"

He looked up and down the street, as if hoping she would appear out of thin air.

"Well, the scream didn't come from inside the bookstore," Tulia said. "I didn't hear anything, and I've been in here ever since I left your donut shop."

"There aren't any tenants above me, so there's only one other place that scream could have come from." He turned to look to his right, to the last unit on the block. "The pet store."

CHAPTER ELEVEN

Tulia could tell Derek was worried. She didn't think he had been joking about trying to get Miranda to go on a date with him; it was obvious he cared for her and had for a long time. With a grim but determined expression on his face, he let the employee entrance slam shut and vanish from her view. She ducked back into the bookstore and hurried around to the front, managing to catch him just as he strode out onto the sidewalk, leaving his donut shop unattended.

Hurrying to catch up, she let the bookstore's front door swing shut behind her. She didn't feel right leaving the store unattended, but if Derek really had heard someone scream, then figuring out what was going on was more important.

"What are you doing?" he asked as she joined him at the pet store's front door.

"I'm helping you," she said. "I told you; my husband's a private investigator. You heard a mysterious scream, and the bookstore owner is missing. What do you *think* I'm going to do?"

He let out a huff of laughter, though his posture was tense as he pulled the door to the pet store open. "In that case, after you," he said.

She stepped through and looked around for Hannah, but the other woman was nowhere in sight. A young man was standing behind the counter with a pair of headphones on, scrolling through his phone. He looked up when they came in and pulled the headphones off of one ear.

"What can I help you with?"

"Is anyone else here?" Derek asked, his tone brusque.

"Owner's in the back feeding the animals," the employee said, putting his headphones back on. "She asked not to be disturbed."

That was unhelpful. Tulia eyed the employee to see if he would stop them. He seemed completely ambivalent to their existence, so she began to walk through the store toward the back, slowing down as she passed the fishtank as if she was admiring it. The employee didn't look up. Derek met her eyes. With a shrug, he nodded toward the back of the store, and they approached the gated-off area together. If this was the sort of employee Hannah hired, no wonder she didn't trust him to care for the animals on his own.

She opened the gate and stepped through into the bird room. The hyacinth macaw seemed to recognize her; he climbed off his perch and up the front of his cage, where he stuck his beak through the bars and made a honking sound at her. She wished she could go to him, but she wanted to make sure no one was hurt first.

"Are you sure you didn't just hear a bird screaming?" she asked quietly.

"I'm sure," Derek said. "I've worked next to this place for three years. I think I can tell the difference by now."

She wasn't so sure about that. A lot of parrots could mimic humans, not just African Greys. But Derek looked determined, so she followed him into the next room with the exotic mammals. The monkeys were shrieking and jumping around in their cages. She shot Derek another look, but he shook his head, his lips pressed together. Not a monkey noise, then.

"Maybe a family emergency came up and she didn't have time to shut the bookstore down before she left," she suggested with a whisper.

"She would never leave the bookstore open and unattended," he said. "She's been working herself to the bone to keep that place open. She would take the two minutes it would cost her to lock the doors before she left."

"Well, she's not back here," Tulia whispered.

Neither was Hannah, for that matter. Tulia eyed the door with all the locks on it. They were all unlocked, which indicated someone was inside. But why would someone have screamed inside the back room where Hannah kept sick animals?

"You can leave if you want, but I need to make sure no one's hurt," Derek said. "I know what I heard. And with Miranda missing…"

He trailed off, but he didn't need to explain. Tulia shook her head, indicating that she was going to stay here with him, and watched as he reached for the door. He didn't knock, he just shoved it open, then jumped back with a curse as something white and fluffy darted out between his legs.

It was a fox, and it raced straight into the bird room.

She heard Derek shout something, but she was already running after the frightened critter, terrified that it would go after the birds. What a fox was doing loose in the back room, she had no idea.

She found it huddling under a cage in the bird room. It had white fur, but she had no idea if it was an Arctic fox or a red fox that had been bred for its color. Derek was still shouting in the other room, but she hated the thought of leaving the fox out here with the birds, so she crept closer and crouched down, holding her hand out tentatively. The fox sniffed her fingers but thankfully didn't bite. Instead, it twisted over so it was lying on its back and pulled its lips back in a submissive sort of grin while it wiggled its whole body. She had no idea how to read fox body language, but she was pretty sure it wasn't being aggressive, so she reached out and scooped it up, marveling at its thick, soft fur. The fox squirmed as she stood up but soon settled in her arms.

With the fox clutched to her chest and the birds screeching at her in alarm, she walked back into the mammal room to see what all the commotion was about. Derek appeared to be struggling to open the door; someone on the other side was trying to shove it closed.

"What's going on?" she asked.

"Miranda's in there!" Derek shouted. "I saw her. She's collapsed on the floor and Hannah won't let me in."

Confused, Tulia opened her mouth to ask if Miranda looked injured when, with a final shove, Derek managed to push the door all the way open, sending whoever was inside stumbling back. Something clattered inside, and she heard a parrot shriek. The sound was joined by a woman's scream when Derek stepped into the room.

Feeling like her hands were tied since she had an armful of fox, Tulia raced over to the door and saw Derek trying to grab Hannah, who had her back to the wall and was trying to fight him off. Miranda was on the floor, groaning softly with a hand pressed to her head. When she pulled it away, her palm was bloody.

A large parrot perch as long as Tulia's arm and nearly as big around lay on the floor next to her.

She had no idea what was going on. She tried to adjust the fox so she could hold it with one hand, but it squirmed in discomfort. She spotted a kennel, like the sort someone might keep a dog in, that had tumbled off a table. She surmised the fox had been kept in there and escaped when someone knocked the kennel down. She hurried into the room and managed to awkwardly straighten the kennel with one hand and put the fox inside, then shut the door before it could escape. With the fox secure, she hurried over to Miranda.

"What happened?" Tulia asked, carefully looking at the gash just above her hairline on her temple.

"She broke in here," Hannah shouted. "I have a right to defend my own property!"

"You could have killed her!" Derek yelled.

A parrot was still screeching, and she glanced up at it, then did a double take. It was another blue parrot, but this one smaller and lighter in color than the hyacinth macaw. She blinked, staring at it. Was that a Spix's macaw? There was no *way*. They were one of the most endangered parrots in the world.

"Get your hands off me!" Hannah shrieked as Derek grabbed her wrist. She lurched forward, shoving her shoulder against his sternum, and he stumbled against the macaw's cage. The macaw lunged forward and sank its beak into his shoulder. He shouted and pulled away, but the pain was enough to make him let go of Hannah, who quickly ran for the door.

"No, wait!" Tulia stood up, but it was too late. Hannah pulled the door shut, and Tulia heard the final sound of the locks on the other side sliding shut, leaving them trapped in a back room filled with illegal exotic animals, while Hannah did who-knew-what on the other side.

Derek tried to yank the door open, then resorted to pounding on it. Tulia turned her attention back to Miranda. "Are you all right? Do you feel dizzy?"

"I don't know. A little," Miranda said.

"What's going on?" Derek asked, turning to them. "What are you doing in here, Miranda? Tulia found the bookstore empty, and I heard someone scream."

"I saw that Hannah was helping a customer load some cages into his car, and she left her employee entrance propped," Miranda said. "I didn't have time to lock the bookstore. It was my only chance to get into the back of her store without her seeing me so I could get proof."

"Proof of what?" Derek said.

Miranda took a shaking breath. "Proof that she's involved with the illegal animal trade. I know it sounds crazy, especially after that book I wrote, but this isn't fiction. And after what happened to Tommy, I had to take the chance."

"What does this have to do with what happened to Tommy?" Tulia asked.

"He was helping me," Miranda said, a guilty look on her face. "While he was helping me with this book, we came in here to look at the animals. He mentioned that some of the animals she had weren't legal to own in Chicago. After that, he spent more and more time in the alley and on the access street, watching what she did after hours. She never paid any notice to him, most people didn't. When he realized that she had even more animals than she let on, some that were illegal to buy and sell on a federal level, he asked me to help him get proof, and I gave him my camera. We wanted to shut her down. She must have seen him taking pictures and realized he was on to her. She killed him, and it was all my fault for getting him involved."

"The camera," Tulia whispered. "That was from you?"

Miranda nodded.

"What are you talking about?" Derek asked.

"Tommy had a camera on him when I spoke to him just a few hours before he was killed, but when the police found him, his camera was gone. He still had the cash I gave him in his pocket, which didn't make sense. If someone mugged him, why wouldn't they take his money, too? But it makes sense now. If Hannah saw him taking pictures of her trafficking animals, then she had a motive to kill him." She turned back to Miranda. "Why did you pretend you didn't know him when I asked you about him?"

"I was worried someone would make the connection between me and him, and I didn't want Hannah to come after me next," Miranda said. "I had no way of knowing if you were connected to her or not. This whole thing has been a nightmare, and now we're trapped in here. What do we do?"

Tulia rose to her feet and took stock of the surroundings. The animals had fallen silent. Her heart ached for them. This must be where Hannah kept the animals she didn't want the general public to know she had, the ones that could get her into a lot of trouble if the authorities learned she was selling them. That Spix's macaw had been stolen from a conservation center or taken from the wild, and she didn't know if the others were legal, or just not the sort of creature that should be sold in a pet shop.

They had to get out of there. Both for their own sake, and to get Tommy and the animals he had been trying to save justice. Her eyes landed on the door.

"The hinges are on the inside," she murmured. "If we can find a way to get the pin out—"

"Then we can take the door off its hinges," Derek finished. "She's got to have something in here. Let's start looking."

They began looking through some plastic storage bins that were filled with animal supplies and got lucky on the third one. Hannah had stored away extra screws for putting together animal cages and had left a screwdriver in with them. The hefty wooden perch Hannah had attacked Miranda with when she found her back here made a convenient hammer.

Taking the pins out of the door hinges was loud work, but if Hannah heard them, she didn't do anything to stop them. When the last pin was out, Tulia helped Derek wiggle the door and the deadbolts out of the frame. Derek carefully leaned the door against the wall, and Tulia winced as the Spix macaw let out a loud squawk, but no one came running.

"Let me go first," Derek muttered.

Tulia wasn't about to fight with him over the privilege of being the first person Hannah saw, so she hung back and helped Miranda as he led the way through the animal rooms. When they reached the gate that led to the main sales area, Tulia saw that Hannah had hung up a sign that read; *Warning: Animals in quarantine. Do not enter.* Derek scoffed and moved the sign aside before pushing through the gate.

She felt like she was stepping into the twilight zone. The pet store was functioning normally, with the same employee she'd seen before sitting behind the counter, while Hannah spoke to someone who was comparing two bird toys. She must have spotted them out of the corner of her eye, because she turned to stare at them and froze for a long second before she uttered a single curse and ran for the door.

"Hey, stop!" Derek took off running after her while Tulia and Miranda followed more slowly.

The customer gave them a wide-eyed look and backed away, and the employee at the counter didn't even glance up from his phone. Derek caught Hannah before she left the store, grabbing her by her arm and turning her to pin her wrists behind her back, so she was facing Tulia and Miranda.

While she tried to convince Derek to unhand her, Miranda straightened her shoulders and strode forward.

"Why did you do it?" she asked. "Why did you kill him? And don't lie to me. We both know you did it."

"Do you have any idea how much some of these animals cost?" Hannah spat at her. "He was going to wreck it all. Wreck *everything*. My business, my livelihood, my reputation. Once this gets out, I'll never be able to work in the animal industry again, and I might even face prison time! Why don't we make a deal? The three of us can work together and share the profits. Miranda, I know you need the money for your bookstore, and Derek, think of all the food you could donate. And you, you like that hyacinth macaw, right?" she asked, looking at Tulia. "You can have him for free. I'll even include a cage."

Tulia wasn't tempted, and by the looks of it, neither were Derek and Miranda. "What was your plan?" he asked. "Let us starve in there?"

"No," Miranda said quietly. "I think it's worse than that. Some of the people Tommy and I saw her meeting after hours looked dangerous, like they might be involved in organized crime. Well, I guess animal trafficking *is* organized crime. I'm pretty sure she had something quicker and more deadly than starvation planned for us. If the people she was working with can smuggle animals into the city, they could smuggle bodies out."

Hannah clenched her jaw and wouldn't look at them, but her silence was answer enough.

"Hey, what's going on?" The employee had finally noticed them. "What are you doing to her? Is one of you *bleeding*? I'm going to call the police."

"Please do," Tulia said. "They have an arrest to make."

She breathed out a sigh of relief as he dialed 911. Tommy would get justice, and Hannah's illegal animal trafficking operation would come to an end. She just wished a man hadn't had to die for the truth to come out.

EPILOGUE

"I always feel sad when we move on to the next location," Olivia murmured, giving the city a wistful glance over her shoulder.

They were in Tulia's sedan, driving together to the long-term parking lot where her RV and Olivia's van had spent the week. The rest of their stay in the city had been uneventful compared to their first few days, and Tulia had spent a lot of her free time with Derek and Miranda as the full extent of Hannah's animal trafficking operation was uncovered. Even though she and Olivia had a busy schedule, Tulia had made the time to help the animal rescue that had stepped up to help the animals move them from their cages to the van that would take them to their new temporary home.

The animals that had been taken from the wild would go into a rehab program, and some of them might be able to be re-released. The ones that couldn't, would be kept in a sanctuary. The other animals would be adopted out into appropriate homes after being looked over by a veterinarian. Tulia knew it was the best outcome they could hope for, and she hoped that the judge threw the book at Hannah. She also hoped that Hannah talked and spilled information about the rest of the animal trafficking ring.

It had been tough to walk away from that hyacinth macaw, but the rescue coordinator had assured Tulia they would vet his new home thoroughly once they found someone who could meet his needs. She knew it was for the best. They barely had room for Cicero and all of his belongings on their road trip. The macaw simply wouldn't fit.

"I know what you mean," Tulia said to Olivia. "I lived hours away from Chicago for most of my life, but I never took the chance to explore it until now. I'd like to go back one day. But for now, I think I've had enough of city living. I want to go somewhere rural, where Cicero can stretch his wings."

"Well, our next stop is Iowa," Olivia said. "I don't think rural is going to be a problem."

Made in the USA
Coppell, TX
10 July 2025